WHERE'S THE UNICORN IN WONDERLAND?

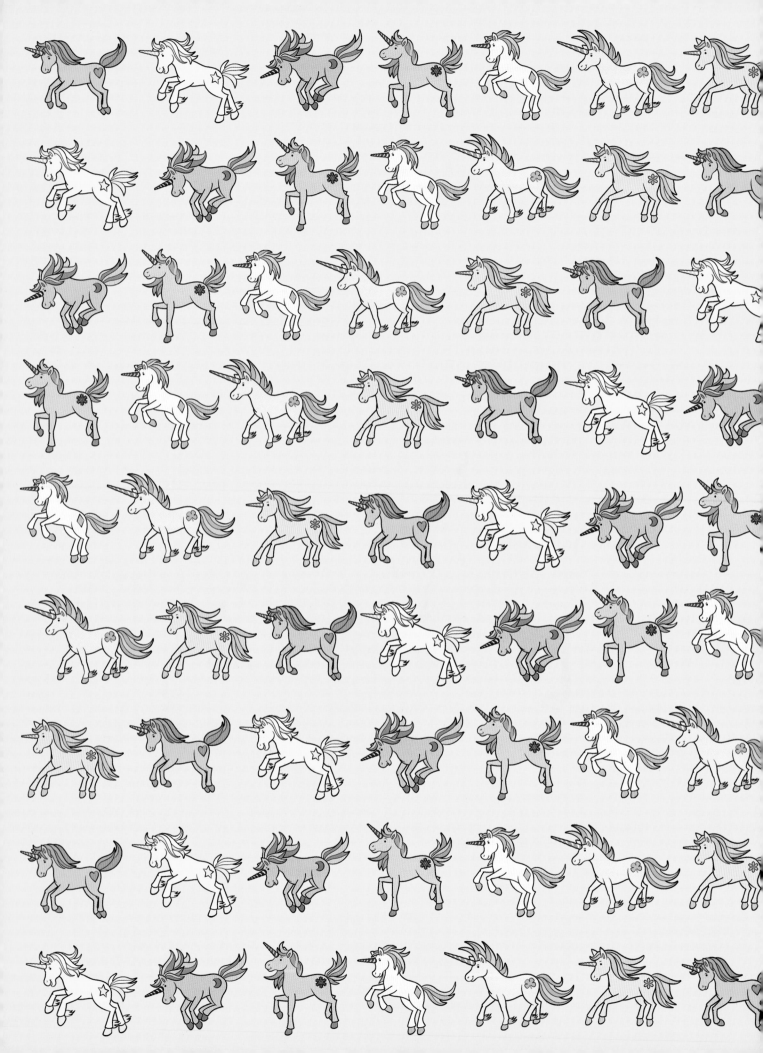

WHERE'S THE UNICORN IN WONDERLAND?

Illustrated by Paul Moran and
Adrienn Greta Schönberg

Written by Frances Evans

STERLING CHILDREN'S BOOKS
New York

INTRODUCTION

The unicorns of Rainbow Valley love to travel and explore new places,
but they have never ventured into the beautiful, wild world of Wonderland.

Wonderland lies far beyond the Rainbow Hills and is home to all kinds of animals and
magical creatures—from mermaids and fauns to phoenixes and centaurs. There are floating
cities in the sky inhabited by dragons, cotton candy forests filled with toybox characters, and
never-ending caves where secretive gnomes and fairies are said to dwell. Ruby and her gang
have decided to go on a tour of its magical kingdoms, and they can't wait to set off!

Can you find all seven unicorns in every scene? They are brilliant at hiding, so
you'll have to search high and low. You can find the answers—plus extra
things to spot—at the back of the book.

THE UNICORNS OF RAINBOW VALLEY

LEAF

Favorite fairy tale: *Hansel and Unicorn*

Favorite color: Elven green

Hidden talent: Flower arranging

Would like to visit: Wonderland's giant maze

RUBY

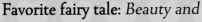

Favorite fairy tale: *Beauty and the Unicorn*

Favorite color: Damask red

Hidden talent: Balancing cupcakes on her horn

Would like to visit: Candy Country

SNOWFLAKE

Favorite fairy tale: *The Piebald Piper of Unicornland*

Favorite color: Dewdrop blue

Hidden talent: Lute playing

Would like to visit: The Snow Queen's wintry realm

BLOSSOM

Favorite fairy tale: *Snow White and the Seven Unicorns*

Favorite color: Tulip orange

Hidden talent: Mane plaiting

Would like to visit: The sunlit Centaur Meadow

LUNA

Favorite fairy tale: *The Little Mermicorn*

Favorite color: Dusk purple

Hidden talent: Dragon taming

Would like to visit: The floating Dragon Castle

STARDUST

Favorite fairy tale: *Rapunzel-corn*

Favorite color: Cowslip yellow

Hidden talent: Tap dancing

Would like to visit: The clockwork city of Mirantibus

AMETHYST

Favorite fairy tale: *Cinder-unicorn*

Favorite color: Clover pink

Hidden talent: Speaks gnomish

Would like to visit: The mysterious Crystal Caves

ENCHANTED FOREST

The border between Rainbow Valley and Wonderland is fringed with magical woods and the unicorns feel right at home here. It's a beautiful summer evening and this clearing is packed with deer, fairies, and woodland creatures.

Ruby wants to try decorating her horn with magical flowers and is going to ask some fairies to help. Snowflake is getting tips from a deer on the best places to visit in Wonderland.

Can you spot all of the unicorns?

CANDY COUNTRY

The unicorns have followed a biscuit road east into Candy Country. The fields are filled with lollipop trees and cotton candy flowers, and this tea-set village is teeming with a crowd of gingerbread people and toybox characters.

Leaf can't wait to have a nibble of a jellybean tree. The beans come in unusual flavor combinations, such as dandelion and sherbet and buttercup and licorice. Meanwhile, Blossom is marveling at the gingerbread architecture.

Can you spot all of the unicorns?

CRYSTAL CAVES

The Shadow Mountains run down
the middle of Wonderland. It would
take days to cross the icy peaks on hoof,
so the unicorns have taken a shortcut
through the Crystal Caves underneath.

The caves are home to gnomes and fairies
of all shapes and sizes. The unicorns are
intrigued by the gems and dragons, but the
gnomes don't have much time to chat—
they've got work to do!

Can you spot all of the unicorns?

ROCKY WILDERNESS

The unicorns have found themselves in a strange wilderness. The landscape is covered in odd-shaped rocks and the only animals around here to ask for directions are magical horses, who don't seem to speak Unicorn.

Luna is having fun racing around the rocks with a group of friendly horses, while Snowflake studies the map in his guidebook to see if he can work out where they are.

Can you spot all of the unicorns?

CLOCKWORK CITY

Next stop is Mirantibus, Wonderland's bustling capital city. The streets are filled with people and creatures from Wonderland's many kingdoms, as well as some incredible mechanical beasts.

Amethyst has gone to grab some breakfast and Leaf is studying the clockwork technology. Ruby, meanwhile, has bought the unicorns tickets for a skyship voyage. The next ship is leaving in ten minutes, so the unicorns don't have long to hang around!

Can you spot all of the unicorns?

FLIGHT ACADEMY

The unicorns have taken a trip on board
a skyship and have landed on the roof of
Wonderland's renowned Flight Academy.
The air is filled with magical creatures,
including flying horses called pegasuses,
stretching their wings and practicing tricks.

Stardust wants to hitch a ride on a dragon,
while Ruby and Luna are watching
the baby pegasuses take their
first flights—they're so cute!

Can you spot all of the unicorns?

DRAGON CASTLE

In the north of Wonderland is the realm of the Hovering Cliffs. This strange, floating land is ruled by a dynasty of dragons who are famed for their knowledge and wisdom.

Luna wants to learn all about the ways of the dragons and is deep in conversation with an old fortune-teller who has foreseen the unicorns' arrival. The rest of the unicorns are enjoying the stunning views—it's not every day you get to see so many phoenixes in their natural habitat.

Can you spot all of the unicorns?

WINTER REALM

The unicorns have arrived in the frozen
domain of the Snow Queen. A dazzling
display of light, known as an aurora, is blazing
across the sky and a crowd of animals and
people are heading toward the palace
to celebrate their queen's return.

Stardust and Snowflake are having a blast
playing in the snow, but the unicorns aren't
used to these sorts of sub-zero temperatures—
they need to head to the castle for a
warming mug of hot chocolate!

Can you spot all of the unicorns?

MAGICAL MAZE

One of the must-see sights of central
Wonderland is this giant labyrinth. The maze
connects Wonderland's many kingdoms,
and it's full of citizens trekking to
and from the magical realms.

Many a tourist has been lost for centuries
within the never-ending maze, so the unicorns
need to choose their path wisely. Leaf's keen
sense of direction has got them this far, but
they're not sure which way to go next. Maybe
one of those goblins can help . . .

Can you spot all of the unicorns?

FAIRY GARDEN

The unicorns have emerged into a topsy-turvy world where they are as small as fairies! This magical garden is full of busy fairies and pixies fluttering between the flowers and playing hide-and-seek with their animal friends.

Blossom is admiring the unicorn-shaped hedges, while Ruby's enjoying wandering between the massive flowers—the scent is heavenly. Snowflake is going to hide from the enormous squirrels. They look a bit peckish.

Can you spot all of the unicorns?

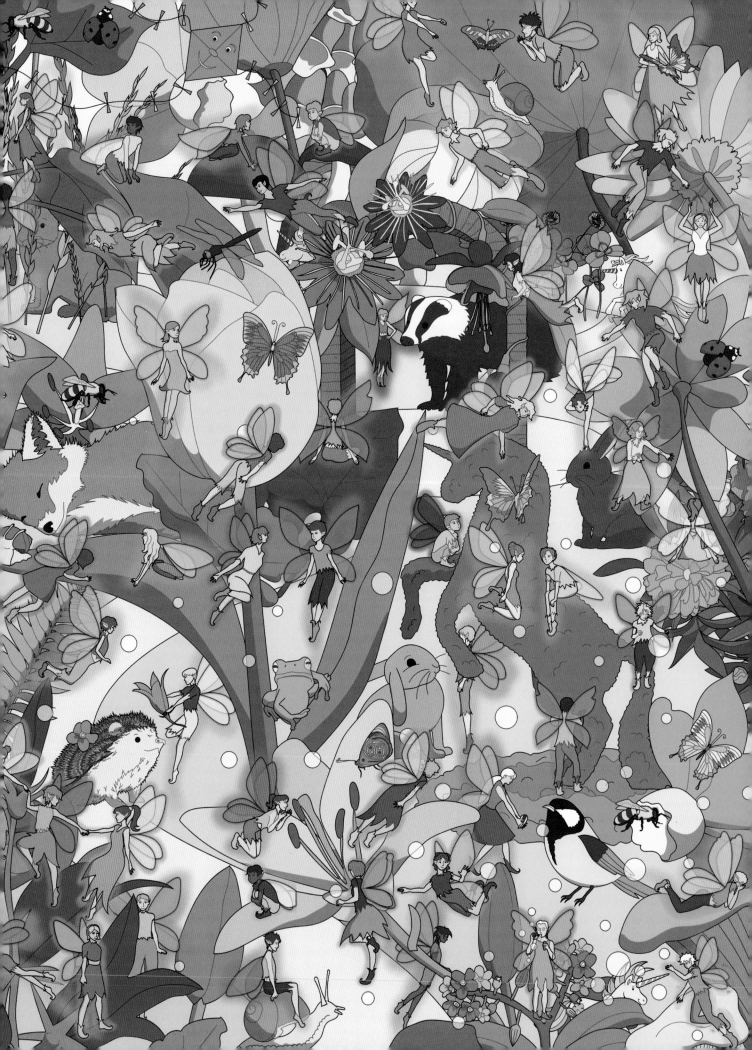

TRANQUIL TREEHOUSE

The unicorns are glad to get some downtime in this beautiful treehouse. It's home to the Timeless Elves, who have lived in this enchanted land for two thousand years (that's about 50 years in elvish terms).

The elves live in harmony alongside many unusual magical creatures. Luna can't wait to say hello to the winged zebras. Snowflake, meanwhile, wants to learn all about the elvish way of life and explore every nook and cranny of the treehouse.

Can you spot all of the unicorns?

CENTAUR MEADOW

The south of Wonderland is home to the centaurs, who are part human and part horse, and the fauns, who are part human and part goat. They love any excuse for a party and have invited the unicorns to a midsummer picnic in a magical meadow.

Stardust and Amethyst are keen to learn a few signature centaur dance moves. Meanwhile, Luna is having fun splashing around in the crystal-clear river. Its waters are said to grant eternal happiness.

Can you spot all of the unicorns?

MISTY SWAMP

The unicorns are passing through the
mysterious Marshspell Swamp. This murky
kingdom is home to sprites known as
will-o'-the-wisps and river horses called
kelpies. Both will trick unwitting travellers
off their paths, so the unicorns need to
keep their wits about them.

While Snowflake marvels at the size of
the toads in these parts, Stardust has decided
to head to the jetty to see if he can get
some directions from the fisherfolk.

Can you spot all of the unicorns?

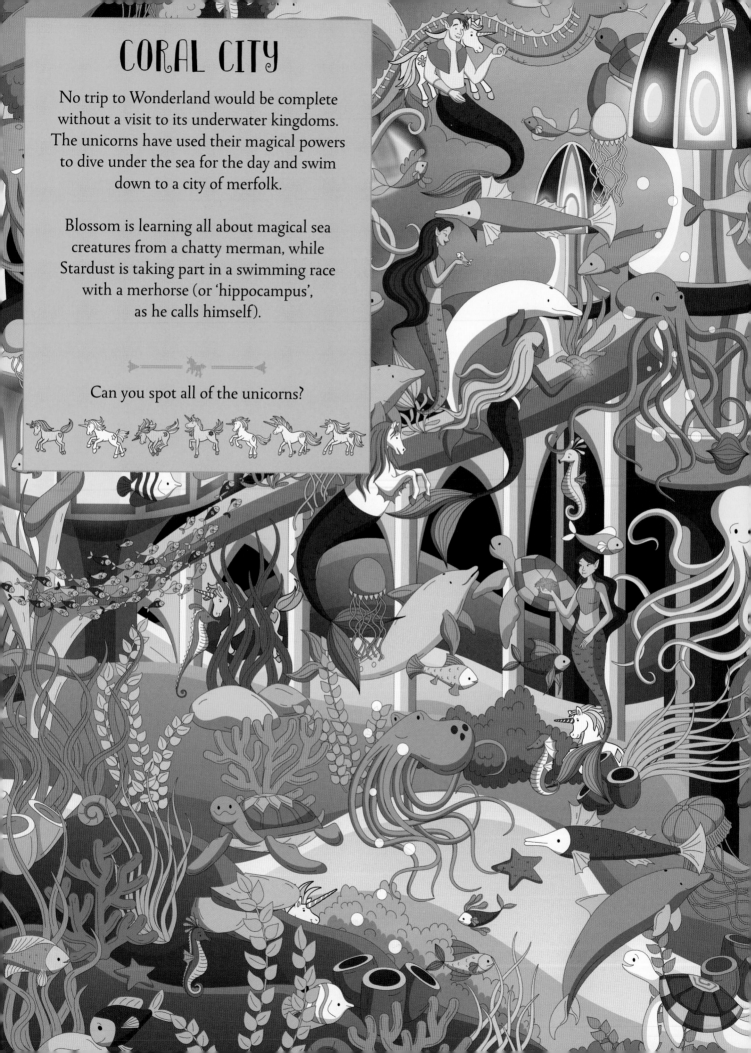

CORAL CITY

No trip to Wonderland would be complete without a visit to its underwater kingdoms. The unicorns have used their magical powers to dive under the sea for the day and swim down to a city of merfolk.

Blossom is learning all about magical sea creatures from a chatty merman, while Stardust is taking part in a swimming race with a merhorse (or 'hippocampus', as he calls himself).

Can you spot all of the unicorns?

JUNGLE RUINS

Next stop are the Ruins of Charm.
This ancient city was once part of a
wealthy kingdom, but the ruler lost
a bet with an enchantress and the
city fell into decay.

The jungle has grown up around the
buildings and today they are home to all
kinds of magical beasts. Blossom is going
to take a closer look at the unusual
plant life and Snowflake is going to
explore the crumbling ruins.

Can you spot all of the unicorns?

MIDNIGHT FOREST

In a forgotten corner of Wonderland lies the Whicketty Woods. The guidebook to Wonderland advises visiting this deep, dark forest 'only if you have a very good reason to and don't mind spiders.'

No-nonsense Ruby leads the unicorns through the twisted thorns, taking care to avoid the giant tarantulas (yikes!). Blossom got distracted and is making friends with a group of travelers who have been lost in the woods for a hundred years.

Can you spot all of the unicorns?

MASQUERADE BALL

It's the unicorns' last night in Wonderland and Princess Eliana of the Peregrine Peaks is hosting a masquerade ball in their honor. The castle grounds are strewn with lanterns and guests have come from all over the land to see the unicorns off in style.

Amethyst is kicking up her hooves with a group of centaurs and Leaf is recounting their adventures to anyone who'll listen. There's still so much of Wonderland to explore—the unicorns will definitely be back someday!

Can you spot all of the unicorns?

ANSWERS

SPOTTER'S CHECKLIST

- A blue stag with flowery antlers ☐
- Two deer in love ☐
- A toadstool house ☐
- A mouse holding a red flower ☐
- A fox stretching ☐
- Six yellow fairies ☐
- A fairy washing line ☐
- A purple bush ☐
- Two owls ☐
- A door in the root of a tree ☐

ENCHANTED FOREST

CANDY COUNTRY

SPOTTER'S CHECKLIST

- A biscuit being used as a surfboard ☐
- A bungee-jumper ☐
- A gingerbread pilot in a plane ☐
- A yellow shark on wheels ☐
- Six Russian dolls ☐
- Three jellybean trees ☐
- Two mice with monocles ☐
- Four giant jelly worms ☐
- A blue toy dog ☐
- An orange pony ☐

CRYSTAL CAVES

SPOTTER'S CHECKLIST

Three sleeping dragons ☐

A fairy in a green dress ☐

A gnome head-first in a barrel ☐

Four gnomes with lit matches ☐

A gnome with an empty barrow ☐

Four gnomes with glasses ☐

Three fairies picking up diamonds ☐

Three barrows filled with giant rubies ☐

One barrow filled with sapphires ☐

A gnome prodding a dragon ☐

SPOTTER'S CHECKLIST

Three orange rock dragons ☐

An airship ☐

A horse playing with a striped ball ☐

A pair of horses nuzzling ☐

A purple horse with a green mane ☐

A red flying horse ☐

Thirteen magical birds ☐

A winged unicorn with a yellow horn ☐

Two blue horses with red stripes ☐

Three blue horses with heart markings ☐

ROCKY WILDERNESS

CLOCKWORK CITY

SPOTTER'S CHECKLIST

Two clockwork peacocks ☐

A robot being wound up ☐

Two clockwork chameleons ☐

A malfunctioning jetpack ☐

Two clockwork unicorns ☐

A twin girl with a pink fan ☐

A woman holding a compact mirror ☐

A robot carrying lots of shopping bags ☐

Two clockwork dogs ☐

A clockwork giant tortoise ☐

FLIGHT ACADEMY

SPOTTER'S CHECKLIST

Three dark blue dragons

A dog

Two chickens

A pirate with a blue bandanna

A woman feeding a griffin

Two green pegasuses

The skyship's anchor

A woman with a purple bonnet

A tower on a cloud

A dragon looking out of a porthole

SPOTTER'S CHECKLIST

A man 'surfing' on two dragons

A nine-headed snake

A pink parasol

A woman petting a fox

A man feeding a phoenix

A snake in a vase

A boy riding a flying unicorn

A phoenix on fire

A monkey falling off a roof

A man reading a scroll

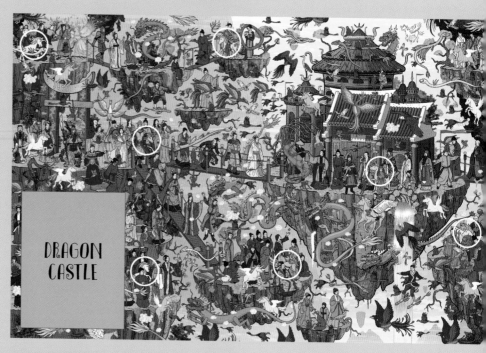

DRAGON CASTLE

WINTER REALM

SPOTTER'S CHECKLIST

The Snow Queen

A child carrying a box

A polar bear lying on its back

Two green coats

Ten snow geese

A woman wearing a blue scarf

A blue snow hare

A sack on a sledge

A gray, leaping fox

A pair of purple snow boots

MAGICAL MAZE

FAIRY GARDEN

TRANQUIL TREEHOUSE

CENTAUR MEADOW

SPOTTER'S CHECKLIST

Three bouquets of daisies ☐

A beetle on a centaur ☐

Four butterflies ☐

A pink blanket ☐

A centaur washing her hair ☐

A faun feeding a swan ☐

A yellow daisy chain ☐

A faun with red hair and beard ☐

A shower of purple flowers ☐

A centaur with white hair ☐

SPOTTER'S CHECKLIST

A wizard with an orange hat ☐

The Swamp Princess ☐

A blue and orange gecko ☐

A purple and yellow frog with a hat ☐

Five nymphs with green hair ☐

A red and purple snake ☐

A pink dancing frog ☐

A turtle with a yellow shell ☐

A man fishing ☐

A green and yellow dragonfly ☐

MISTY SWAMP

CORAL CITY

SPOTTER'S CHECKLIST

Two mermaids with red hair ☐

A yellow and pink seahorse ☐

A merman holding a shell ☐

Two white and green dolphins ☐

A blue shell ☐

Two red starfish ☐

Two purple octopuses ☐

A turtle with a red rim on its shell ☐

A glowing green sea flower ☐

Two merhorses ☐

SPOTTER'S CHECKLIST

Two unicorn statues ☐

A purple and green lion on a rock ☐

A winged cat washing itself ☐

A red toucan with a purple beak ☐

A blue winged cat ☐

Four dragonflies ☐

Four red parrots with green beaks ☐

Four orange dinosaurs ☐

Three blue and yellow hummingbirds ☐

Three big cats yawning ☐

SPOTTER'S CHECKLIST

A green dragon ☐

A wolf pup pulling on a dress hem ☐

Two cauldrons ☐

An owl family ☐

An elf prince with a rose ☐

Two girls in blue picking flowers ☐

The wolves' burrow-den ☐

A man in a mask ☐

A yellow cat ☐

A knight on a black horse ☐

MIDNIGHT FOREST

MASQUERADE BALL

SPOTTER'S CHECKLIST

A glass slipper being returned ☐

Three fauns playing pipes ☐

An enchanted rose ☐

Six grey rabbits ☐

A centaur treading on a man's toe ☐

Two unicorn topiary sculptures ☐

A mermaid catching a fish ☐

A man with a very long nose ☐

A group of breakdancers ☐

A blue parasol ☐

STERLING CHILDREN'S BOOKS
New York

An Imprint of Sterling Publishing Co., Inc.
122 Fifth Avenue
New York, NY 10011

First published in Great Britain in 2020 by Buster Books,
An imprint of Michael O'Mara Books Limited, 9 Lion Yard,
Tremadoc Road, London SW4 7NQ, England

First Sterling edition published in 2021.

ISBN 978-1-4549-4292-4

Distributed in Canada by Sterling Publishing c/o Canadian Manda Group,
664 Annette Street, Toronto, Ontario M6S 2C8, Canada

For information about custom editions, special sales,
and premium and corporate purchases, please contact
Sterling Special Sales at 800-805-5489
or specialsales@sterlingpublishing.com.

Manufactured in Singapore

Lot #:
2 4 6 8 10 9 7 5 3 1
12/20

sterlingpublishing.com

Designed by John Bigwood
and Zoe Bradley

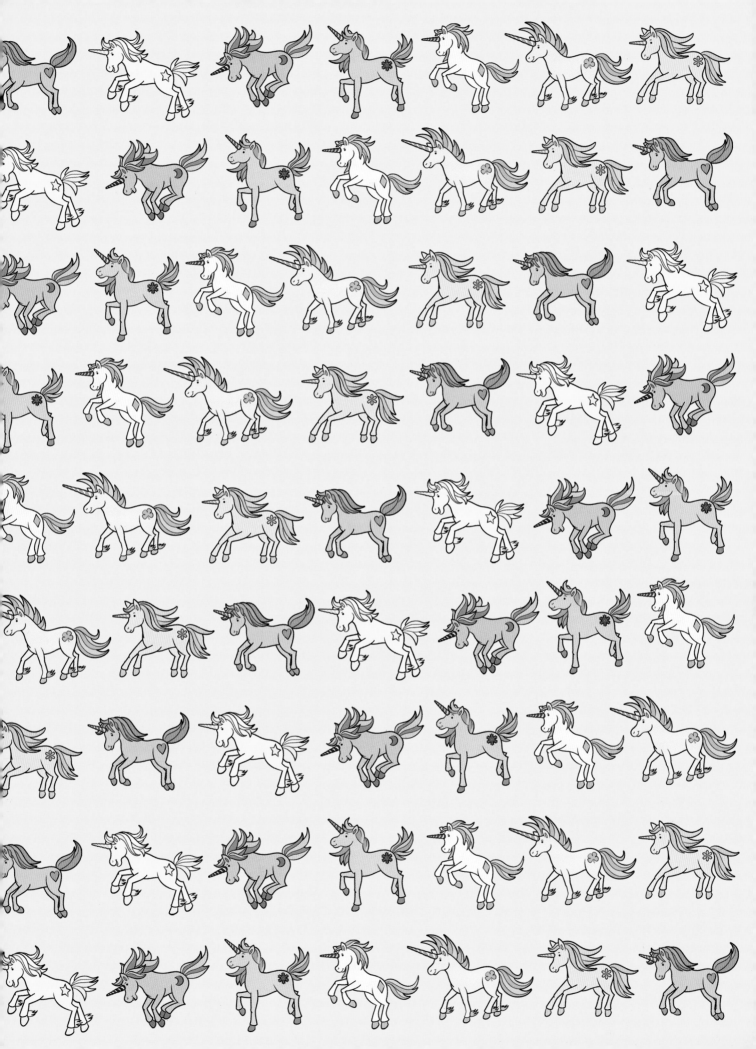